Hey, You're NOT Santa!

by **Ethan T. Berlin**

illustrated by **Edwardian Taylor**

Orchard Books
An Imprint of Scholastic Inc.
New York

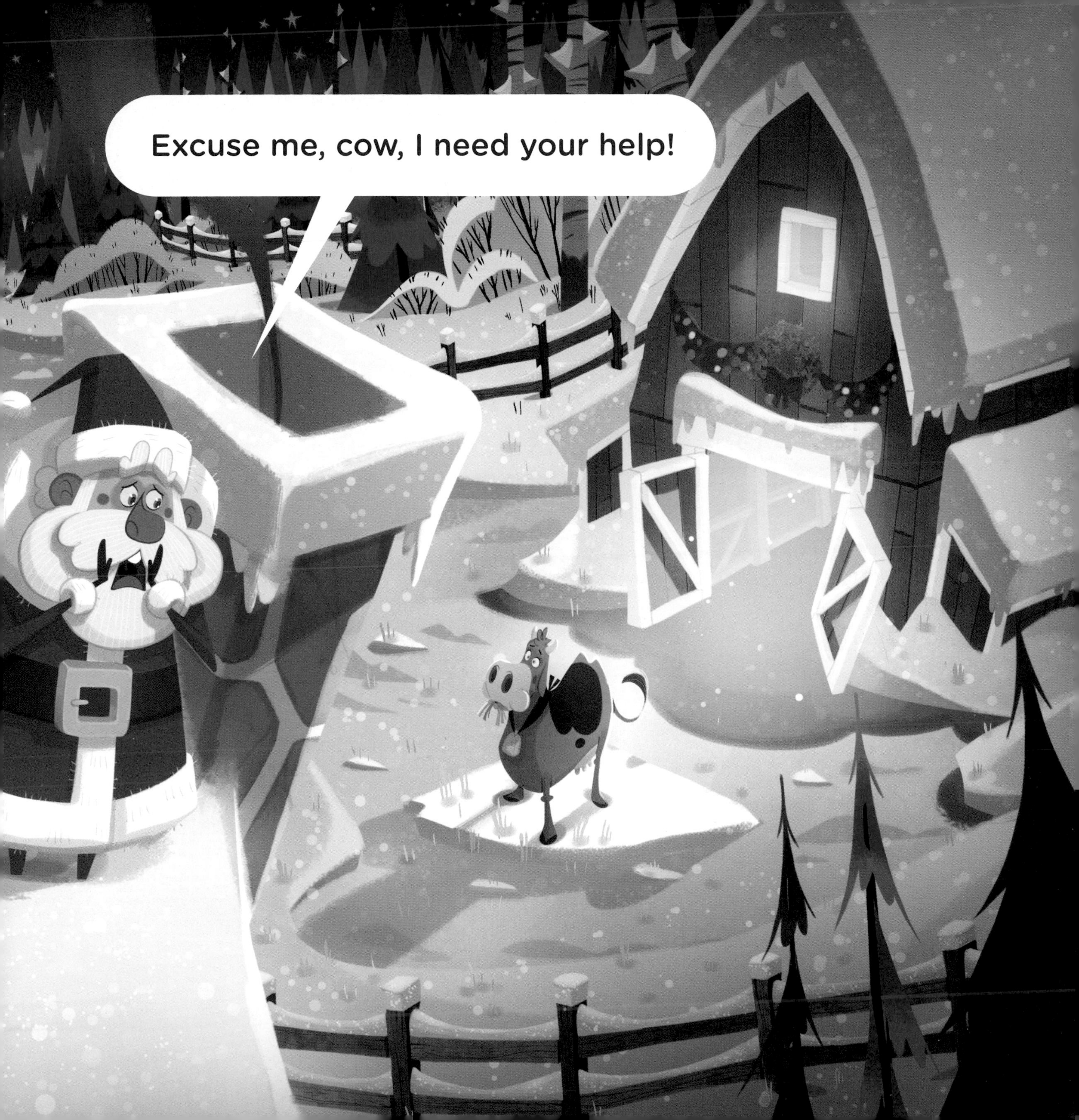
Excuse me, cow, I need your help!

The boy in that house is waiting up to see me, but I've forgotten some of his presents.
Could you pretend to be me while I fly back to the North Pole?

Thank you! And please don't let him know that you're not really Santa. I don't want to ruin the magic for him.

Yes, it is I, Santa! You can tell because I say that thing Santa says, **"Moo-moo-moo, Merry Christmas!"**

Right, that's what I meant. **Ho-ho-ho-mooooo!**

Hey, are those cookies for me?
Yes! But unfortunately we're out of milk.

I have never heard about Santa giving milk to kids.

Well, I've started this new thing where I bring presents AND really fresh milk.

Oops. Yes. But, um, first I have to check my list to see if you were **Naughty** or **Grass**.

You know, it used to be Naughty or Nice, but I changed it to Naughty or Grass, because I love eating grass and leaves and **trees**.

Delicious! Thanks for putting this out for me.

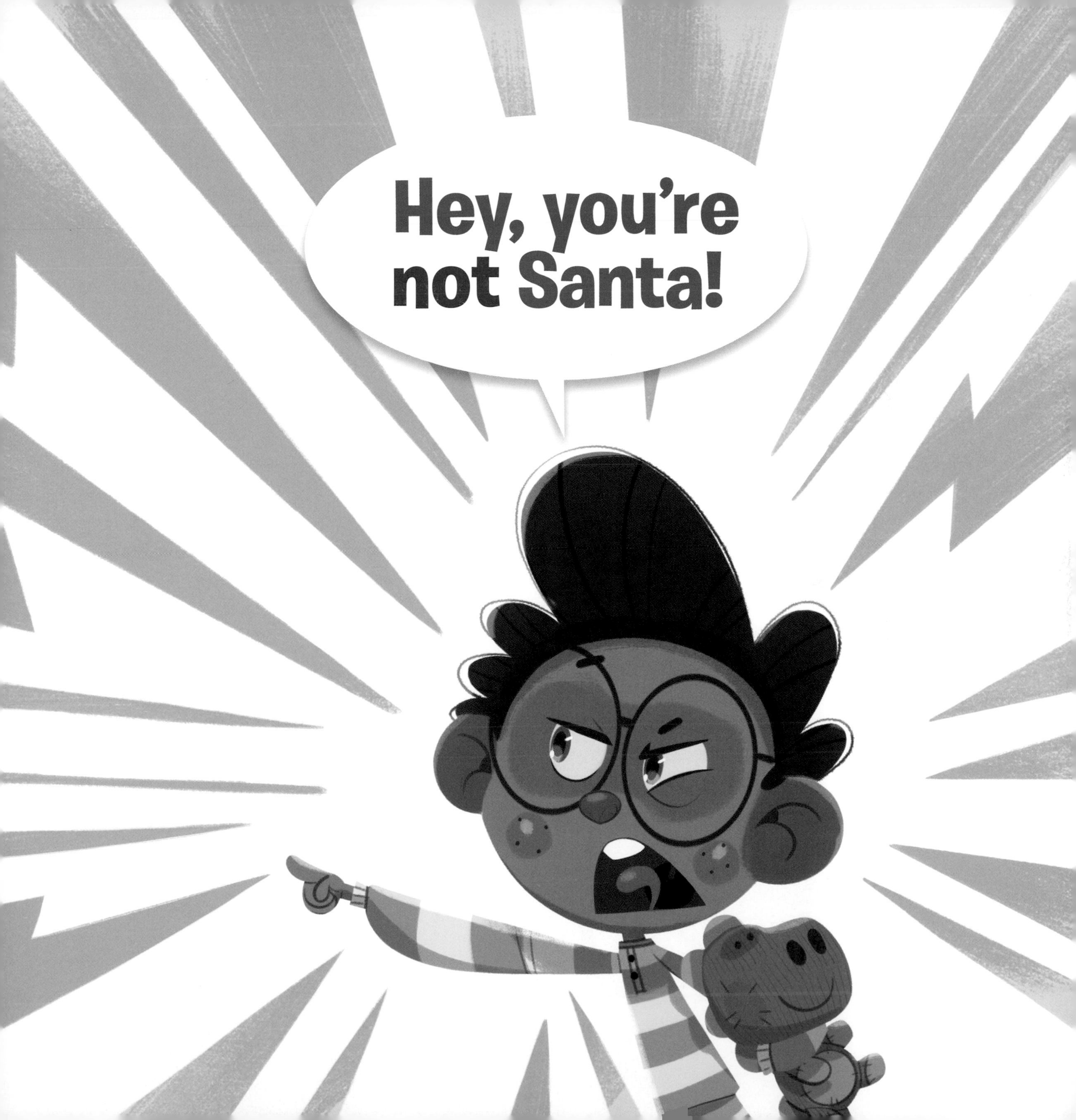
Hey, you're not Santa!

Reindeer? Right, um . . . there's Dasher, and, uh, Prancer. And, of course, Mooooooooo-dolph.
DASHER

I'm sorry, you're not Santa.
Santa knows the names of his reindeer!
Santa does not eat Christmas trees!
And Santa DOES NOT make milk!
YOU'RE NOT SANTA CLAUS!

I can't keep this up anymore. You're right. I'm not Santa. I'm a cow, and I was just helping Santa because . . .

. . . I had to go back to the North Pole to get you even more presents since you were so NICE this year!
KID

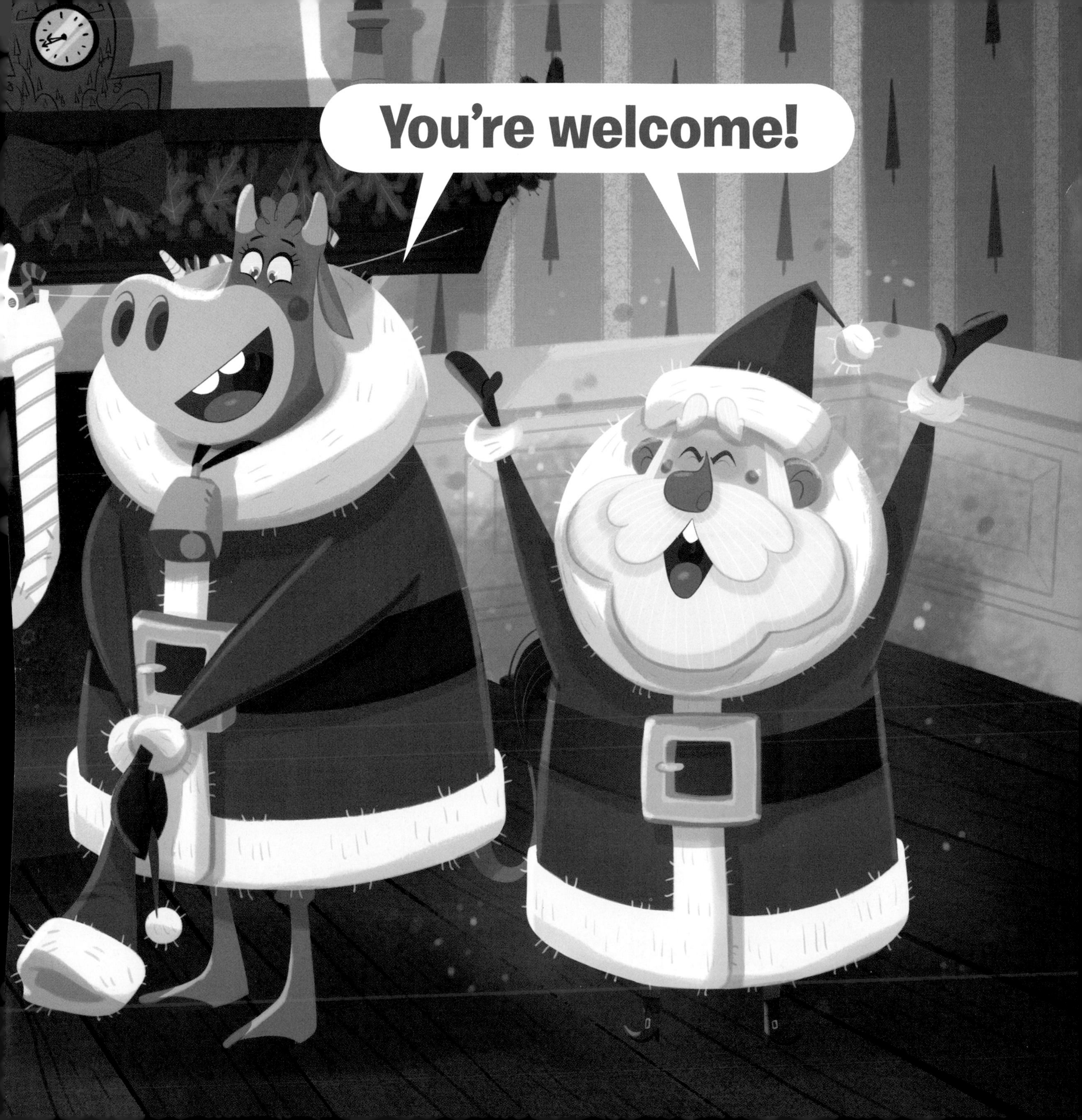
You're welcome!